The Clumsy Cow

For my siblings, you know why.

First published 2004
Evans Brothers Limited
2A Portman Mansions
Chiltern St
London W1U 6NR

Text copyright © Evans Brothers Ltd 2004
© in the illustrations Lisa Williams 2004
Reprinted 2005

British Library Cataloguing in Publication Data

Moffatt, Julia
     The Clumsy cow. - (Zig zags)
     1. Cows - Juvenile Fiction
     2. Children's Stories
     I. Title
     823. 9'2 [J]

ISBN 0237527901

Printed in China by WKT Company Limited

Series Editor: Louise John
Design: Robert Walster
Production: Jenny Mulvanny
Series Consultant: Gill Matthews

The Clumsy Cow

by Julia Moffatt

illustrated by Lisa Williams

Evans

Buttercup the cow was very clumsy.

When the farmer milked her, she knocked the bucket over.

"Oops-a-daisy," said Buttercup.

Buttercup went for
a walk.

10

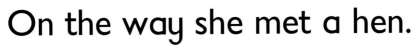

On the way she met a hen.

"Hello," she said.

Then Buttercup
slipped and...

...trod on the nest and broke some eggs.

"Oops-a-daisy,"
said Buttercup.

Buttercup was hungry.
She ran to get her lunch...

...but she bumped into all the other cows.

"Oops-a-daisy," said
Buttercup.

None of the animals
wanted Buttercup
near them.

"I wish I wasn't so clumsy,"
cried Buttercup.

23

"Cluck, cluck!" cried the hens.

24

she fell on top of
a big fox!

"Goodness me," said the farmer.

28

Why not try reading another ZigZag book?

Dinosaur Planet   ISBN: 0 237 52667 0
by David Orme and Fabiano Fiorin

Tall Tilly   ISBN: 0 237 52668 9
by Jillian Powell and Tim Archbold

Batty Betty's Spells   ISBN: 0 237 52669 7
by Hilary Robinson and Belinda Worsley

The Thirsty Moose   ISBN: 0 237 52666 2
by David Orme and Mike Gordon

The Clumsy Cow   ISBN: 0 237 52656 5
by Julia Moffatt and Lisa Williams

Open Wide!   ISBN: 0 237 52657 3
by Julia Moffatt and Anni Axworthy